THE
BLUE JACKAL

Written by **Shobha Viswanath**
Illustrated by **Dileep Joshi**

EERDMANS BOOKS FOR YOUNG READERS

GRAND RAPIDS, MICHIGAN • CAMBRIDGE, U.K.

Juno the jackal lived deep in the jungle
with his cousins and aunts and one very old uncle.
Whenever the moon shone out full and bright,
the jackals — and Juno — howled all through the night.

Juno was terribly puny and lean,
and the bigger jackals were really quite mean.
They laughed at him cruelly for being so skinny,
calling him names, like sissy and ninny.

And even though Juno would hunt with the pack,
the jackals wouldn't give him so much as a snack.
At feeding time they would eat themselves sick,
leaving poor hungry Juno just bare bones to lick.

When one day his hunger was too much to bear,
he climbed up a hill to see what was there.
From far up above, Juno hungrily gazed
at a small quiet town where a herd of cows grazed.

Baby goats played and hens ran around.
Roosters crowed boldly; pigs rolled on the ground.
The jackal drooled at the thought of the treat.
So many animals, all ready to eat!

He waited until the sun had gone down.
Then when all were asleep, he crept into town.
He sniffed out the hens and snuck through the dark,
but then through the night came the sound of a bark!

The big village dogs were out on the prowl.
And when they saw Juno, they snarled and growled.
They charged at Juno from every side.
The poor jackal panicked — where could he hide?

He darted away and blindly he fled
toward the village dyer's small darkened shed.
He leapt through a window set rather high,
falling — splash! — in a big vat of indigo dye.

The dogs couldn't find him and gave up the chase.
But Juno, still frightened, didn't move from his place.
All through the night his fur soaked in the dye,
turning him blue as an afternoon sky.

Early next morning when Juno slipped out,
the people still slept and no dogs were about.
He dashed away quickly into the woods,
running as fast as his little legs could.

Deep in the forest, Juno slowed down.
His fur was now blue — it was no longer brown.
The animals saw him and cowered in fear.
"What is this creature?" whispered the deer.

"He's blue as the ocean and bluer than me!"
the proud peacock cried from the top of the tree.
"So royal a blue can mean only one thing.
This beautiful creature must be our king!"

Juno looked down, and found it was true:
his fur was a strange and wonderful hue.
It shone out so blue in the morning's clear light
that all of the animals scattered in fright.

And then a thought struck.
Juno called out with charm,
"Come back, my dear subjects,
I mean you no harm.
Yes, I am your king,
your lord and your master.
I come from the heavens
to rule ever after."

The animals came back and bowed to their king.
"Your majesty, ask us to do anything!"
"Drive out the jackals!" said Juno. "Away!
Inside this forest, no jackal must stay!"

When the jackals were banished, Juno lay back.
His new subjects brought him a meal, then a snack.
Juno felt pleased, sitting high on his throne.
His hunger was gone, and his worries had flown.

Many such days did pass in delight,
until a full moon rose up one night.
The silvery moonlight, so pure and divine,
sent a powerful shiver up the blue king's spine.

And what was this sound that Juno could hear,
this faraway song that still felt so near?
His family was howling away at the moon.
Forgetting his act, Juno joined in the tune.

The animals heard Juno.
At first they were curious.
But then they were angry,
and soon they were furious!
Their king was a jackal,
his true colors shown.
They roared and chased Juno
away from his throne.

. . .

Many moons later,
the rains flooded down.
The blue washed away
and left Juno brown.
But no matter what troubles
his life might now bring,
he never forgot
that he once was a king.

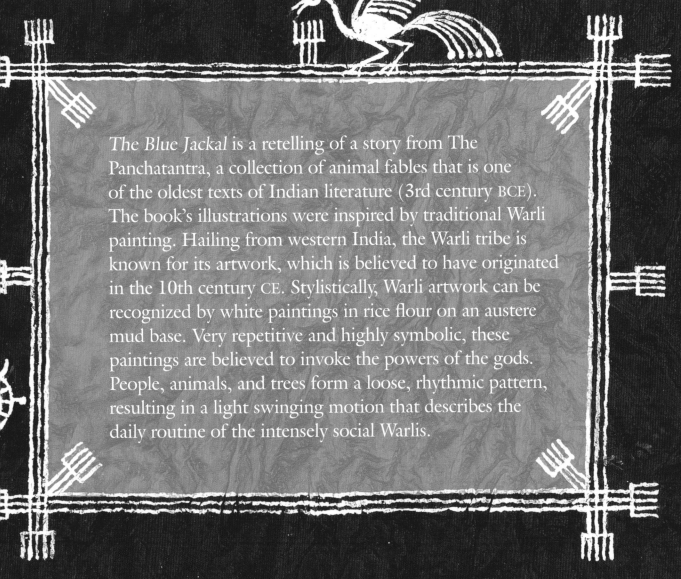

The *Blue Jackal* is a retelling of a story from The Panchatantra, a collection of animal fables that is one of the oldest texts of Indian literature (3rd century BCE). The book's illustrations were inspired by traditional Warli painting. Hailing from western India, the Warli tribe is known for its artwork, which is believed to have originated in the 10th century CE. Stylistically, Warli artwork can be recognized by white paintings in rice flour on an austere mud base. Very repetitive and highly symbolic, these paintings are believed to invoke the powers of the gods. People, animals, and trees form a loose, rhythmic pattern, resulting in a light swinging motion that describes the daily routine of the intensely social Warlis.

Shobha Viswanath is the cofounder and publishing director of Karadi Tales in India. She has previously published books with Puffin and Scholastic. Shobha's work is focused on reclaiming a place for Indian literature for children.

Dileep Joshi graduated from Sir JJ School of Art in Mumbai and has worked as a freelancer with several advertising agencies. He has illustrated books for Scholastic India and Karadi Tales.

First published in the United States in 2016 by
Eerdmans Books for Young Readers,
an imprint of Wm. B. Eerdmans Publishing Co.
2140 Oak Industrial Dr. NE
Grand Rapids, Michigan 49505
P.O. Box 163, Cambridge CB3 9PU U.K.

www.eerdmans.com/youngreaders

First published in 2014 by
Karadi Tales Company Pvt. Ltd.

3A Dev Regency
11 First Main Road Gandhinagar Adyar Chennai 600020
www.karaditales.com

23 22 21 20 19 18 17 16   9 8 7 6 5 4 3 2 1

Manufactured at Tien Wah Press in Malaysia, first edition

ISBN 978-0-8028-5466-7

A catalog listing is available from the Library of Congress